The HUEYS in WHAT'S the OPPOSITE?

For Leni

www.oliverjeffersworld.com

First published in hardback in Great Britain by HarperCollins Children's Books in 2015
First published in paperback in 2016

10 9 8 7 6 5 4 3 2 1

PB ISBN: 978-0-00-742072-8
PB & CD ISBN: 978-0-00-816530-7

HarperCollins Children's Books is a division of HarperCollins Publishers Ltd.

Visit our website at: www.harpercollins.co.uk

Printed and bound in China

The HUEYS in WHAT'S the OPPOSITE?

 OLIVER JEFFERS

HarperCollins *Children's Books*

"Is it yes?"

"Uh... no!"

"Let's try an easier one...

What's the opposite of up?"

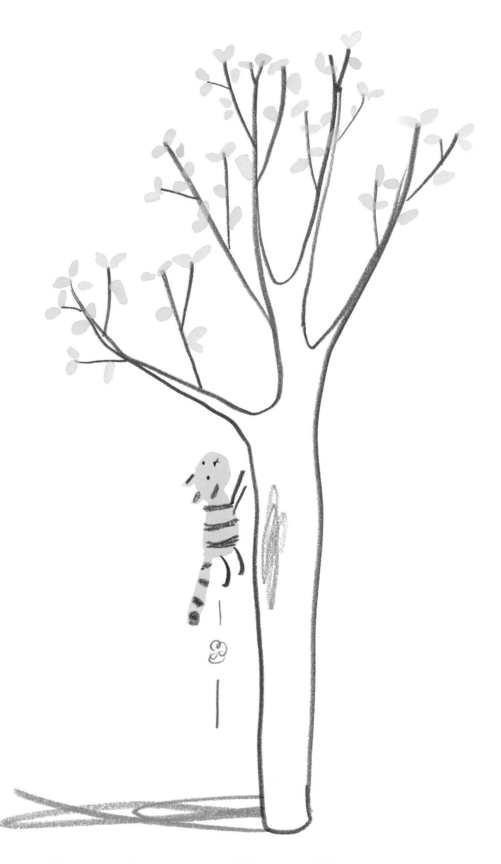

And the opposite of high…

Here...

and there!"

Cold... **hot.**

Unlucky...

lucky…

unlucky again.

On...

good DAY!

How do?

off.

Big...

small.

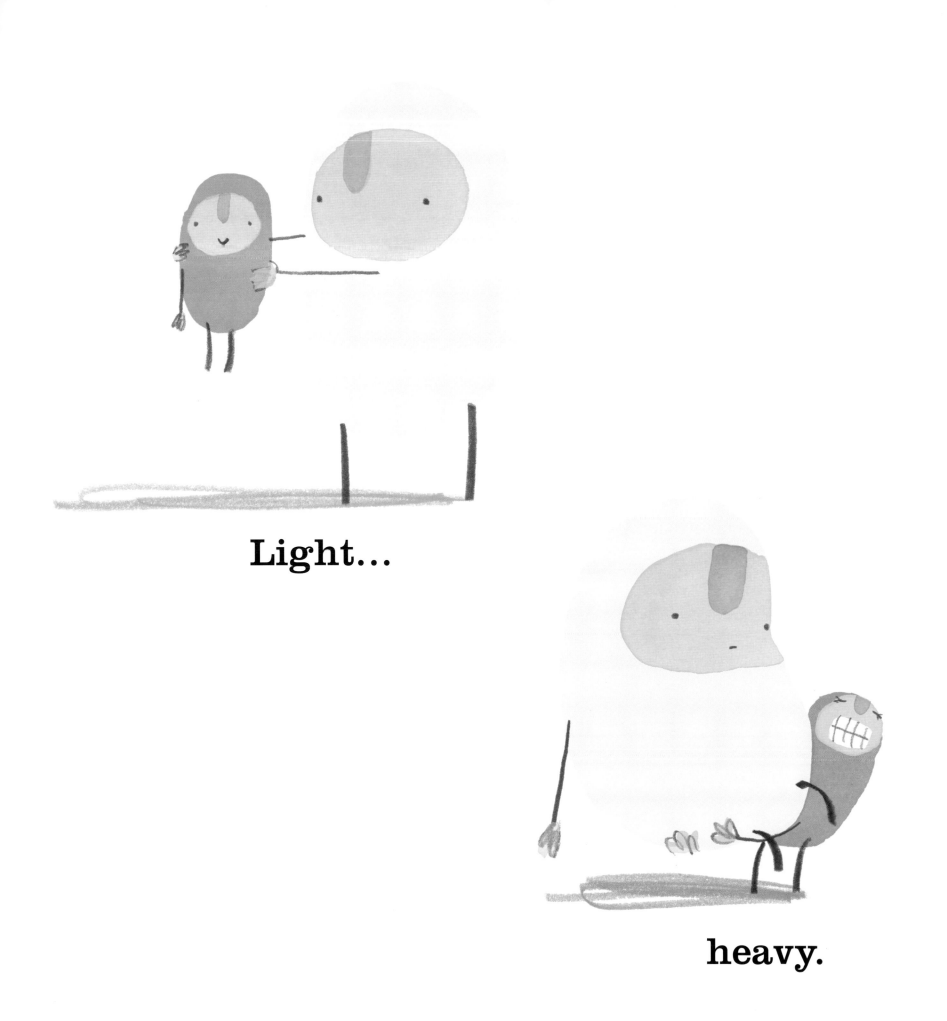

Light...

heavy.

Happy...

sad.

Now for a trickier one...

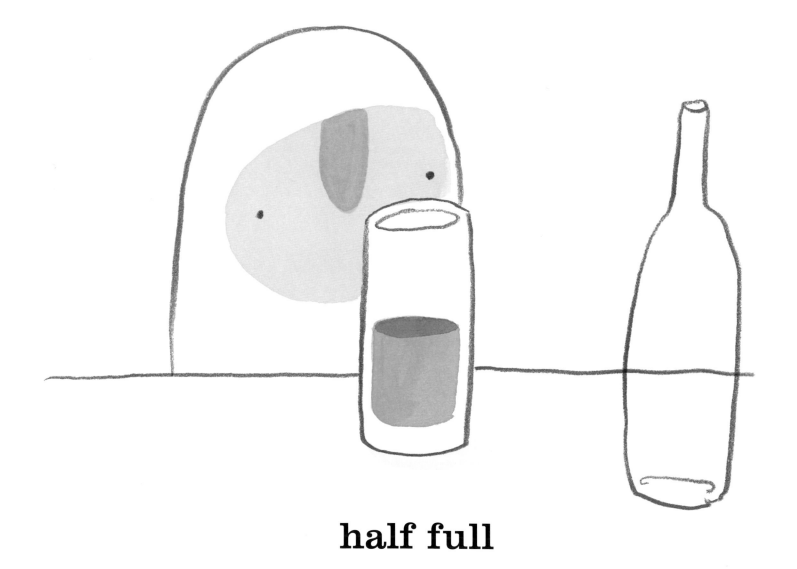

half full

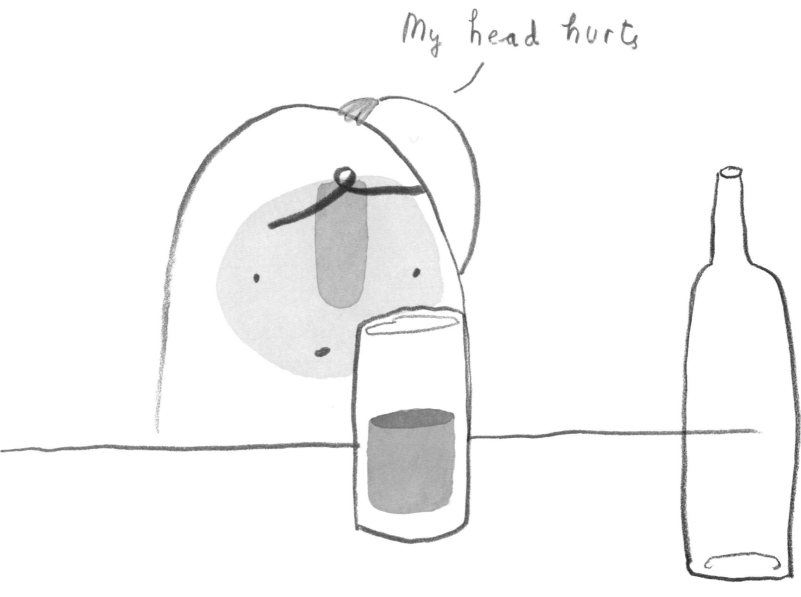

half empty.

All right, let's finish with something simple..."

"So...
what IS the opposite
of the beginning?"

"Oh, yes!
It's..."

Also look out for these brilliant picture books!